SISTERS

Also by Lily Tuck

The Double Life of Liliane
The House at Belle Fontaine
I Married You for Happiness
Woman of Rome: A Life of Elsa Morante
The News from Paraguay
Limbo, and Other Places I Have Lived
Siam: or, The Woman Who Shot a Man
The Woman Who Walked on Water
Interviewing Matisse: or, The Woman Who Died Standing Up

SISTERS

A NOVEL

LILY TUCK

Atlantic Monthly Press
New York

*Published simultaneously in Canada
Printed in the United States of America*

FIRST EDITION

ISBN 978-0-8021-2711-2
eISBN 978-0-8021-8920-2

Atlantic Monthly Press
an imprint of Grove Atlantic
154 West 14th Street
New York, NY 10011

Distributed by Publishers Group West

groveatlantic.com

17 18 19 20   10 9 8 7 6 5 4 3 2 1

To Jessica and Michelle

First and second wives are like sisters.
—Christopher Nicholson (*Winter*)

SISTERS

We are not related—not remotely.

In the old days it was not unusual for a man, after his wife had died—but *she* is not dead—to marry his wife's younger sister. Already she had come into the household to care for her dying sister and then remained to care for the children, do the cooking and the housework. She was a useful and necessary presence. Think of Charles Austen, Jane Austen's brother, think of the painters William Holman Hunt and John Collier; all three married their dead wives' sisters despite the fact that until 1907 there was a ban in England, the Deceased Wife's Sister Marriage Act, on such marriages—known as sororate marriages. In the Hebrew Bible, Jacob's marriage to the sisters Rachel and Leah, forebears of the Twelve Tribes of Israel, is also such an example.

And we don't look alike. *She* is blond, fair-skinned, big-boned, and taller than I. I have also seen photos of her as a young woman and I have to admit *she* was lovely. Truly. Now, *she* is a handsome woman in a slightly ravaged way. Her best feature is her nose—a Grecian nose, I think they call it—the sort that has no bridge and starts straight from the forehead. Like Michelangelo's *David*.

I am dark and petite.

According to Wikipedia, Michelangelo's *David* is 5.16 meters or nearly 17 feet tall and weighs 5,660 kilos or 12,478.12 pounds.

In one of the photos I saw of her as a young woman, *she* is pushing a baby carriage—an old-fashioned big black baby carriage—down a city street in Paris. The street is shaded by large chestnut trees and, in addition to pushing the carriage, *she* is holding a little dog on a leash. The dog, a white-and-black terrier, is straining at the leash.

"Heel," *she* could be telling the dog. "Heel, damn it," but the dog pays her no attention.

"She didn't like dogs much," my husband once told me. "She liked cats. I hate cats," he adds.

"I love dogs," I told my husband.

At first I had pictured her in a house full of cats. Cats everywhere. Cats stretched out on the sofa, on the chairs, lying on top of the kitchen table, sitting on the windowsill licking themselves clean, eating from bowls on the floor. A mess. I was reminded of the book I had just read about poor Camille Claudel, Rodin's discarded mistress, made mad by neglect and poverty. Her apartment on the Quai de Bourbon in Paris, a home for feral cats.

Sometimes when I could not sleep—many nights, actually; I have insomnia—instead of counting sheep, I tried to count the number of times during their marriage that they had made love. I was just guessing of course but, for argument's sake, let's say that for the first two years—they were both young, in their twenties—they made love nearly every night so call that one thousand fucks; then the third and fourth year, maybe they made love only two or three times a week so let's call that three hundred fucks and then, of course, it got less. Also, *she* had had two kids in between, so again, if they made love two or three times a week for the next eight or nine years that made it about eight hundred more fucks and, probably, toward the end of their marriage, they didn't fuck at all. So I was guessing that *she* and my husband fucked about two thousand times during their marriage. As for me and my husband—we were older, he was in his forties—we

fucked a lot the first year and after that we fucked
only once or twice a week and usually only on Sunday mornings.

I was told that *she* was musical. I was also told—by the same person, a person who knew her quite well before her marriage, a fellow student, in fact—that *she* could have had a career as a concert pianist. *She* spent two years in Philadelphia studying at the Curtis Institute of Music, which has one of the most competitive and storied piano performance departments in the world.

"I remember how she said she would never forget studying with Eleanor Sokoloff and Seymour Lipkin—especially Seymour Lipkin," the same person who knew her quite well told me. "And how Lipkin told her that as a pianist she had a moral responsibility to the composer to play what the composer thought and felt and not what she felt like playing. She told me she would never forget that. Funnily enough," the person said, "I haven't forgotten that either."

Once married, however, *she* gave it up.

Did he dissuade her? I wondered.

I have a career, but I am not a pianist or an artist. My career gives me some financial freedom, it gets me out of the house, but it is not all consuming. If I had to give it up tomorrow, it would not matter much. I am not passionate about my work.

I also could not help wondering if *she* resented him for making her give up her career—if that is what he did or if that is what he, in his most charming and persuasive way, suggested.

And did her resentment contribute to their getting divorced? My guess is that the reason they got divorced was not due entirely to her giving up the piano.

I also have to say here that as far as music is concerned I have a tin ear.

"She and I took lessons with Mrs. Sokoloff on her Bösendorfer," the fellow student who had known her added.

"Her what?"

"A Bösendorfer piano has ninety-seven keys instead of eighty-eight. The extra nine keys are at the bass end of the keyboard, and on Mrs. Sokoloff's piano they were hidden underneath a hinged panel mounted between the piano's conventional low A and the left-hand end cheek so that you would not accidentally hit them. Now, instead of concealed by a panel, the extra keys are painted black to differentiate them from the standard eighty-eight."

As for her children—a boy and a girl—we get along now. But when their father and I first married, I had worried. I was nervous. The boy, thirteen at the time, seemed indifferent to me. The girl, slightly older, was hostile. Not having children of my own, I tried too hard to please them. I wanted them to like me—to love me—and I allowed them liberties that, in retrospect, I should not have. For instance, I never said anything when they did not make their beds or when they threw their wet towels on the floor in the bathroom. I also did not say anything when they left their dirty dishes for me to take to the sink and wash. As time passed, however, I relaxed and acted more honestly. I spoke my mind.

I think they eventually understood that instead of trying to replace their mother, I was supporting her.

Unfortunately, the boy got into drugs for a while. Looking back, I should perhaps have said something to him, but at the time I did not want to interfere.

"Does your mother have a cat?" I asked him once.

High, his pupils dark and dilated, he laughed. "*Meow, meow.*"

I asked his daughter the same thing.

"She had two—Simone and Nelson. Unfortunately, Nelson, named for Nelson Algren, died last week. She's still very upset."

Nelson Algren famously wrote: *Never sleep with a woman whose troubles are worse than your own.*

People, of course, took sides. A lot of them blamed my husband for the divorce and some of them probably blamed me as well. But their blame was not justified. I had nothing to do with the divorce. Yes, it was true that I had met him while he was still married, but by then he and his wife were not getting along. In fact, as he later confessed to me, he and his wife had not had sex in over six months.

We met at a friend's dinner party and I remember how he told the hostess that he was very sorry but his wife had suddenly been taken sick with the flu and could not attend, although, as it turned out, the part about his wife being sick was not true. They had argued and at the last minute she said she was not going out for dinner and was staying home. As a result, the dinner party hostess had had to change the table seating at the last minute and I ended up sitting next to my future husband. The host was sitting on my other side and since I had known him since our college days I remember I did not feel intimidated or nervous. I even remember what I talked to the host about: we talked about how another classmate had moved to Silicon Valley and how neither one of us, no matter how financially beneficial that job might be, would ever want to do that. I actually have quite a good memory, or so I have been told, and I also remember what I was wearing—a pair of black tuxedo trousers (the kind with a satin stripe down the side) and a white silk blouse with a V-neck—and I can remember exactly what we ate at that dinner party: smoked salmon on toast to start with, then duck à l'orange, wild rice, and French string beans, then salad with assorted cheeses, and a crème brûlée for dessert. All of it delicious.

Preheat oven to 300 degrees.

In a small saucepan, combine cream, vanilla bean, and granulated sugar; place over medium heat and stir occasionally, until bubbles start to form around the edges of the pan. Do not boil. Remove from heat and set aside.

Whisk egg yolks in a large bowl; while whisking constantly, slowly add hot cream mixture to egg yolks. Continue whisking until—

But I promised myself never to copy down a recipe.

The last time I saw her was at her daughter's wedding, a grand affair for which my husband paid a small fortune. He was happy to and money never mattered much to him, for which I admired him; also, he liked his about-to-be new son-in-law. So did I. The wedding was formal—caterers, flowers, printed invitations—and a success. The reception took place at an elegant club in midtown and my guess was that there were over two hundred guests—most of them young and most of them his daughter's friends, which was as it should be. My husband wore his best blue suit, a white silk shirt, and a silver tie while I had gone out and bought a new dress. An expensive, designer navy polka-dot silk dress on which I got many compliments—even my husband said: "*Très chic!*" More important, his daughter looked beautiful. Since her father had offered to pay for the dress, we had gone together to several bridal boutiques and after many hesitations and concerns, on her part, she had finally chosen a beautiful satin gown with a pannier skirt—at least that was how the saleslady described it. The gown, I remember, had a series of—maybe thirty in all—tiny silk-covered buttons up the back and when she had tried it on, I had done them up for her. Not easy. On the day of the wedding, I imagined how her mother had had to do up all those buttons for her daughter.

During the dinner, while we were all sitting at our respective tables (I was seated, not at the head table with the bride and groom and my husband, but at an adjacent table with relatives—the aunts and uncles—of the groom), and after the toasts, there was music and dancing. My husband first danced with his daughter—after she had danced to Frank Sinatra's "Fly Me to the Moon" with the groom—and it made me happy to watch them. I know how much he loved his daughter. Next, he danced with his former wife and, to be honest, my heart sank as I watched them glide across the floor effortlessly to Frankie Valli's "Can't Take My Eyes Off of You." My husband was holding her tightly around the waist and *she* had her hand high up on his back, nearly touching his neck. I had to admit to myself that they looked good together. Eventually the groom's uncle who was sitting next to me and who had traveled all the way from Madison, Wisconsin, for the wedding, had asked me to dance.

Our own wedding was small. My sister and her husband came from Austin, Texas. Eloise and Harold. Eloise is a few years younger than I am and we have never been close. Less so once she got married and she had kids, reasons I suppose for her to act superior to me. I've met her kids. Her kids are surly and overweight.

We had dinner together the night before the wedding. My husband had booked a table for us at an expensive French restaurant and I noticed how Eloise took obvious greedy pleasure in her food—since I last saw her, she too had gained weight—and Harold seemed to be enjoying several glasses of wine, a Mouton Rothschild. But while we were waiting for our dessert—Eloise had ordered the tarte tatin—she followed me into the ladies' room and voiced her objections.

"He's divorced," she said.

"I know he's divorced," I answered from the adjoining stall.

"He might not be suitable," she said.

"Suitable how?" I asked, flushing the toilet.

"He's got two teenage kids."

"So? They have a mother."

"Have you met the mother?"

"Yes," I lied as I washed my hands.

"What is she like?"

"She's very nice."

I was in several relationships before I married my husband. Two of them serious. The first was in graduate school with a man named Tim. Tim and I were both getting our master's in communications at Tulane University; he wanted to go into television and I was not sure what I wanted—marketing, I said. We rented a house with some other students in the Garden District of New Orleans. We drank a lot, smoked pot, did a bit of cocaine, and collected beads at Mardi Gras. I can't remember why we broke up—we just did, and I moved back East. I was on my own for a while, I had a good job marketing tea and soups for a large Dutch company, and eventually I started going out with my boss. Of course, my boss was married and it was all tricky and difficult especially since I fell in love with him. Mostly we met on business trips to Amsterdam, where we would stay in the same hotel but book separate rooms. It was lovely and romantic until his wife found out. Someone in the office must have suspected and told her. She threatened to divorce him and he had to swear to her never to see me again which he did and which broke my heart.

I never told my husband any of this. And despite my own reservations about speaking of it, I have to admit that his lack of curiosity about my love life was not flattering.

Once while we were making love, my husband called out her name instead of mine.

Sometimes I wondered whether *she* had had boyfriends before they got married. Or was she still a virgin? I also wondered whether men find deflowering a woman for the first time thrilling and satisfying. Or do they think it an onerous task?

I should have asked him but didn't.

He had good taste and dressed well—he wore bespoke shirts made in England. And I liked how he smelled. A lot of men I have known have a sour smell, especially during sex. I liked that he could make me laugh—like the time we sat in my backyard garden and he said he felt as if he were in Holland.

Before we got married, he sent me flowers every single day.

The first time I saw her was from the living room window. *She* had bicycled over to our apartment with her daughter. *She* wore a long paisley skirt and wooden clogs.

"Was that your mother?" I asked her daughter, although I knew it was.

Somewhere I read that either alder, birch, syca-more, willow, or beech—woods that won't split—is chiefly used to make clogs.

I don't know why but I have been trying to think of his daughter's husband's uncle's name—the man I danced with at her wedding. I actually danced with him several times and each time he became more and more unruly. First he had put his hand on my butt, then he had tried to kiss me on the mouth right there in the middle of the dance floor. He must have been drunk. It was embarrassing, but I don't think anyone noticed. My husband did not notice. The man's name was on the tip of my tongue. But what I remember most about the evening was how I had felt abandoned and insignificant.

"Did you ever hear her play?"

"Who?" my husband asked.

"Your wife—I mean your ex-wife," I answered.

"Of course," my husband said. "Of course, I heard her play. I've already told you she played beautifully. She could have had a career as a pianist."

After dinner, we were watching television in the den—a live broadcast of a musical evening at the White House. President Obama and his wife, Michelle, were sitting in the front row; they both looked happy. Stevie Wonder was playing "As" on the piano.

"What did she play?" I continued.

"Classical stuff—you know—Mozart, Beethoven, Bach, Chopin . . ."

"Oh, I love Chopin," I said.

"I thought you said you had a tin ear?"

"I do, but I like listening to music. I just can't tell specifics like what key things are in. I just . . ."

My husband looked at me and frowned. "The point is?" he asked.

"Music can transport me."

My husband snorted.

Stevie Wonder finished playing and, smiling, Obama and Michelle clapped wildly.

I imagined her sitting at a grand piano, the one with the nine extra keys, in a huge concert hall; *she* swayed a little as *she* played and as her feet pressed down on the pedals. Her arms were bare and her blond hair shone in the light. Next to her, attentive, a young man was turning the pages of the music score. When *she* finished the piece *she* stood up and took a bow. The audience clapped wildly. *She* smiled and put her hands together to her chest to acknowledge the audience. The audience continued clapping.

"Encore, encore," someone in the audience shouted. Others took up the shout. "Encore!"

My old boyfriend Tim sent me an e-mail saying he was coming to town and he hoped to see me and catch up. He suggested we get together for a cup of coffee.

Sure, I thought. Why not?

She and I spoke at her son's graduation. His school was located in a small, pretty New England town and the day before the graduation my husband and I drove up to the town from the city. It was getting late as we were driving on the Mass Turnpike—he was going eighty-five miles an hour and the speed limit was sixty-five miles an hour—and we got stopped by a state trooper and the state trooper gave my husband a ticket. The ticket cost over two hundred dollars and my husband was furious. But worse still, the trooper made him get out of the car and take a Breathalyzer test as well as walk a straight line with his hands behind his head counting from one hundred-and-one down to eighty-one backward and by odd numbers. Not only was my husband furious but he was humiliated, so much so that it ruined the weekend for him (no doubt for his son as well). During the entire next day while we were at his son's graduation, he kept telling everyone he spoke to—his son's teachers, the other parents, whoever would listen to him—about how unfair the speeding ticket was and how humiliating it was to have to take the Breathalyzer test and how he was going to speak to the Massachusetts state attorney who was a friend of his to make sure that the state trooper, whose name he had taken down, was going to spend the rest of his life regretting this. It was embarrassing.

He even told his ex-wife about the speeding ticket and I remember how *she* just smiled and shrugged.

One hundred-and-one, ninety-nine, ninety-seven,
ninety-five, ninety-three . . .

Occasionally, on the weekends when her children were staying with my husband and me, *she* telephoned and asked to speak to one of them.

Usually I was the one who was home and who answered the phone.

"He's out," I would tell her.

"He's out with his dad."

I never said he's out with my husband.

Usually they were out biking—biking for miles up the Hudson—all three of them good-looking, coordinated, athletic.

She lived across the city from us. Maybe a mile or two as the crow flies and, as a result, our paths did not cross a lot. But once, because her son had left a book at our house and had called saying he needed it right away for class, I took the crosstown bus and went to her apartment. The building was a high-rise and had several entrances and it took me a while to find the right one. Her apartment was on the eleventh floor and when *she* opened the door for me I could see *she* was surprised to see me. I, too, must have stared at her, and probably *she* thought I was staring at her outfit — black tights and a white T-shirt—because *she* said, "I do tai chi."

Stupidly, I said, "Oh, I do yoga."

Standing in the doorway, I could see into the living room which was painted white and looked airy and uncluttered. The furniture consisted of a single sofa, a coffee table, a few chairs, and a grand piano along the far wall. Out of the living room window I could see the river and the New Jersey shore.

"Do you want to come in for a minute?" *she* asked.

And instead of saying "Yes," I got embarrassed and lied. "Thanks, I have to run," I said. "I have an appointment downtown."

I handed her the book and, without another word, I turned and left.

"I'm sorry about Nelson, your cat," I might have said.

On the bus, on my way to her apartment I had tried reading her son's book:

In mathematician Felix Klein's posthumously published memoir Development of Mathematics in the Nineteenth Century *(1926), Klein says of Hermann Grassmann that unlike "we academics [who] grow in strong competition with each other like a tree in the midst of a forest which must stay slender and rise above the others simply to exist and to conquer its portion of light and air, he who stands alone can grow on all sides."*

Grassmann's mathematics was outside the mainstream of thought; read by few, his great work, Die lineale Ausdehnungslehre (The Theory of Linear Extension, 1844), *was described even by Klein as "almost unreadable." Yet this book, more philosophy than mathematics, for the first time proposed a system whereby space and the geometric components and descriptions could be extrapolated to other dimensions.*

His son was musical, too. He played the guitar and was in a rock band at school. (I know a lot of kids play the guitar and are in bands.) Maybe I felt sorry for him because his father was always hard on him—harder than he was on his sister.

"He's a late bloomer," I said.

"Don't give me that late bloomer shit." My husband started to get angry. He never liked being disagreed with.

"He's good at math." I tried again. "Programming and all that technical computer stuff."

My husband did not answer.

"Maybe you should try to talk to his mother," I said.

"About what?" my husband asked.

I didn't answer.

On a few occasions, making an excuse to myself—fresher organic produce, hard-to-find Italian virgin olive oil—I would again take the crosstown bus to shop in her neighborhood. I would go to Fairway, the big supermarket that was just a few blocks from her apartment. Slowly I would push my cart down the aisles and study the clementines in season, the avocados, the hydroponically grown tomatoes; or I would stand in front of the cheese counter as if trying to decide which kind to buy—the Camembert or the Roquefort?—hoping to catch a glimpse of her. Sometimes, I stood around for such a long time without buying anything that the person behind the counter would get impatient and ask: "Miss, can I help you with something?"

Once while I was standing in front of the saltwater tank watching the live lobsters inside it, I saw what I thought was her reflection in the glass.

"Hi," I said, turning around quickly and calling out her name.

Only it wasn't her, and the woman, who was blond but otherwise did not look like her, frowned at me and said, "Fuck you, too."

"Have you ever had bouillabaisse?" his daughter asked me during dinner one night.

"No—bouilla—what?"

"Bouillabaisse. It's a French soup prepared from fish stock and different kinds of fish and shellfish, like mussels and clams. It comes with a sauce made with cayenne, saffron, garlic—"

"The best bouillabaisse I ever had was in Marseille," my husband said, interrupting. "I went there with your mother during a holiday—*la Toussaint*—when I was at INSEAD. It was October, months before you were born," he added, winking at his daughter.

"My mother makes it occasionally—it's really good," his son said.

"I'll never forget the restaurant," my husband continued, "it was right on the harbor. The old port. Nothing fancy and full of locals. I wish I could remember the name of it. *Chez* someone . . ."

"My mother got the recipe from a Julia Child cookbook. She says it takes her all day to make it," his daughter said.

"I wonder if the restaurant is still there," my husband continued. "I would go back in a heartbeat.

"*Chez Maurice*!" he almost shouted. "That's the name of the restaurant. A miracle I remembered it."

My guess, only a few months pregnant, *she* threw up the bouillabaisse in the street next to the old port.

Next morning, first thing, I went to the bookstore around the corner from where we live and
bought Julia Child's *Mastering the Art of French Cooking*, Volumes 1 and 2.

The fish Julia Child's suggests to use for a
bouillabaisse are halibut, eel, winter flounder, hake,
baby cod, small pollock, and lemon sole. Shellfish,
she writes, are not necessary but add glamour and
color to the soup.

One of the arguments my husband and I had was over a dog. I had seen an ad at our bookstore— the bookstore owners are animal lovers and their cat sits on a pile of best sellers all day. Right away I called and was told that all but one male had already been sold. "Please," I begged, "can you keep him for me for a few days while I check with my husband? My husband is out of the country on business," I lied.

"Poodles are very smart. They are the second-smartest breed of dog after the Australian sheep-dog," I said, trying to convince my husband. "And the kids, too, like dogs."

"Who's going to walk the dog?" my husband asked. "Who is going to pick up the shit?"

My husband traveled a lot on business. However, instead of going to Europe and to glamorous cities like Paris, London, and Berlin, he mostly traveled in the United States and Canada. He went to cities like Dallas and Houston and San Francisco and Seattle and to cities in the Midwest like Des Moines and Saint Louis. Usually, he was away only a day or two and often, when he returned home, he was tired and hungover.

"Those lousy hotels," he said. "I can never get enough sleep."

"All those client dinners," I said.

"And missing you," he said, putting his arms around me.

My husband genuinely liked women.

Every so often my husband talked in his sleep. Usually the words were incomprehensible or they made no sense. Or no sense to me.

Turn off the water! he once called out. *It's too hot, I tell you!*

In the morning, I questioned him.

"What were you dreaming about last night?" I asked. "You were yelling about the water being too hot."

He shrugged. "Too hot? I don't remember."

"Were you taking a shower in your dream?" I persisted.

"I told you I don't remember."

One night, he repeatedly called out a woman's name. Not her name. *Lena.*

"Who's Lena?" I asked him in the morning.

"Lena? I don't know any Lena."

After a moment, he said, "Lena Horne. Maybe I was dreaming about Lena Horne."

"I love the chicken masala and the vegetable samosas, the bread, too—what's it called—naan," I told his daughter.

We were sitting in an Indian restaurant waiting for her father.

"Dad is always late," his daughter said.

It was her birthday and we were celebrating it.

"One day, I want to go," I said. "To India, I mean."

"My mother wants to go to India, too," his daughter said. "She wants to go to the state of Tamil Nadu."

"Tamil Nadu?" I repeated as my husband rushed into the restaurant full of apologies for being late and keeping us waiting.

"What shall we order?" he said sitting down. "Something spicy—I like spicy Indian food. And happy birthday, darling," he added.

"You know what I didn't realize?" his daughter once said to me.

She and I get along well. Very often I feel as if she could be my daughter, too.

"No, what?"

We were sitting in the living room after dinner; her father and brother were watching television in the den. A basketball game. We heard them yell excitedly from time to time.

"I didn't realize that my mother was happier once she got divorced from Dad. She sort of came into her own."

"How could you tell?" I asked.

"Well, for one thing, she wants to travel and, for another, she started playing the piano again. She loves that."

"What are you two talking about?" my husband asked, coming into the room during the commercial.

"Nothing," we both said.

I dreamed—not that I went back to Manderley—
that I was in a big city like Calcutta or Bombay in
India. I was sweating and the streets were packed
with people pushing and shoving and beggars, too,
who clutched at my skirt and tugged at my arm and,
in the dream, I became more and more frightened
and at one point I started to run when all of sudden
I saw her. *She* was dressed in a bright green sari and
she had a red dot painted on her forehead. Relieved
to see someone I knew who could perhaps help
me, I called out her name, but *she* kept on walking
as if *she* did not know who I was. Then I woke up.

In the morning, when I started to tell my
husband about how I had had a dream that upset
me—without mentioning her—he interrupted me,
saying, "I can never remember my dreams."

In the dictionary I looked up the red dot worn by Hindu women called a *bindi*. Traditionally, it is worn by married women; widows are not allowed to wear red, but they can wear a black dot; young women can wear a *bindi* of any color except black. The *bindi* is known as the third eye chakra. Worn between the eyebrows, where the pineal gland lies, it is said to retain energy and concentration.

In addition to sleeping pills, I also kept Valium in my medicine cabinet. I rarely took the Valium—only if I went to the dentist or if I flew. But when I went to take a Valium—I was on my way to the dentist to have a cavity filled—I noticed that there were a lot fewer pills in the little vial than I remembered. Instead of about twenty pills, there were only six. How so? I wondered. The housekeeper, Margarita, would not have taken them—she speaks little English and I would be surprised if she knew what the generic name *diazepam* signified. If his daughter had wanted some Valium I am sure she would have asked me, which left his son. Valium, I know, is a helpful downer if you are high on drugs.

Margarita came to work for us after Dona left. Apparently, Dona had been working for my husband's family for years, ever since the children were little, and everyone, except me, loved Dona. Dona left soon after I moved in. She never actually confronted me with any problems, only I felt them. And a few times, I had to point out to her that the furniture was not polished properly—rings left on the tables—and once I found hairs on top of the drain in one of the shower stalls. I tried to be as diplomatic as possible but at the same time I had to assert myself. I also could not help wondering about what *she* was like as a housewife—did *she* not care that things were not clean and tidy? Then I found pieces of my grandmother's china sauceboat in the garbage. The sauceboat was part of a Meissen china collection my grandmother had brought over from Europe and given to me. Each cup, plate, and saucer as well as the sauceboat was decorated with little pastel flowers and each piece had the two blue crossed swords—the Meissen authenticity mark—incised in the back. Needless to say I was and am very fond of this china for both sentimental and aesthetic reasons, to say nothing of how valuable the china is. Anyway, I confronted Dona with the pieces and of course she denied breaking the sauceboat. The next week she told me she was leaving. Her excuse was that she had to babysit for her new grandchild. I paid her for an extra two weeks and let her go. Afterward I complained to my husband about Dona and told him about finding the broken pieces of the sauceboat in the garbage.

"I'm pretty sure she was lying," I told him.

"She wasn't," my husband said.

"How do you know?"

"I broke the sauceboat."

"What?"

"I was reaching for something on the shelf and it fell out. Sorry," he said. "And I didn't know you cared so much about it."

"I do and why didn't you tell me?" I asked, close to tears.

"I forgot," he said.

"I'll get you another," he added.

The other thing I remembered about his daughter's wedding—besides my husband dancing with his former wife and the groom's drunken uncle dancing with me—was running into her in the ladies' room. I was just coming out of a stall when *she* went into it—I remember holding the door open for her at the same time that we gave each other a little smile, a nervous little smile.

"Oh, hello," *she* said.

"Hello," I said back.

And those were the only two words we exchanged. However, looking back on this encounter, I can't help laughing at the thought of her sitting on the same toilet seat I had just vacated—only it should have been the other way around.

Ha ha.

Suspended for a term from his school for drinking alcohol, his son worked at the local public library.

"All I do is shelve books," he told me. "It's boring. I can't even read. When I graduate, I am going to travel—"

"If you graduate," his father interrupted, walking into the room.

"And don't you encourage him," he added, shaking his head at me.

"Congratulations," I said to her. "You must be very proud."

"A relief," *she* answered with a slight smile. "I didn't think he would make it all the way to graduation."

The ceremony over, parents and students were standing together outside on the school's manicured lawn.

"I did," I said.

She looked at me without speaking.

"He's a very intelligent and talented boy," I said to fill in the silence. "I'm very fond of him," I added since *she* still had not spoken.

"He's fond of you, too," *she* finally said.

"The majority of bond trading is done between institutions," my husband told us. At dinner, after a few glasses of wine, he was more loquacious and expansive and more apt to try to explain what he did all day. "And depending on the number of bonds being bought, the price can be negotiated."

"What about junk bonds?" his son asked.

"Junk bonds get a bad rap. Even if they have a credit rating below the BBB by Standard and Poor's because they have a higher risk of default they still will pay a higher interest rate. The right junk bond fund can be a smart move for a diversified portfolio."

"What about the mortgage-backed securities?" His daughter was more numerate than her brother and more up-to-date on the news.

My husband raised his eyebrows at her and said, "I can't believe you are really interested." Then before she could answer, he continued, "MBSs are bonds secured by home and other real estate loans.

They are created when a number of these loans are pooled together. For instance, a bank offering home mortgages might round up ten million dollars' worth of such mortgages. That pool is then sold to a federal government agency or a government-sponsored enterprise or to a securities firm. Another group called 'private label' MBSs are issued by subsidiaries of investment banks—like ours." He paused, poured himself more wine. "Unlike traditional fixed-income bonds, most MBSs give bondholders monthly—not semiannual—interest payments. The reason for this is that homeowners pay their mortgages monthly, not twice a year. The big difference between Treasury bonds and MBSs is that the Treasury bond pays you interest only, and at the end of the bond's maturity you get a lump-sum principal amount, while an MBS pays you both interest and principal. This of course means that when the MBS matures you don't get a lump-sum principal payment. Do you follow me?"

His daughter nodded while his son and I said nothing.

I was curious about the two years he studied at INSEAD—Institut européen d'administration des affaires. The school was located outside Paris in Fontainebleau and he had to commute from the small apartment they rented off Avenue Foch. (Avenue Foch must have been where the photo was taken of her pushing the baby carriage while holding the little terrier on the leash.)

"Did you learn to speak French?" I asked him.

"Enough French to order a meal and get around."

And what about her? My guess was that *she* picked up French in no time because *she* was musical and had a good ear.

Parlez-vous?

I have always wanted to go to Paris—France is a lot closer than India.

One time, my husband asked me to go with him to Montreal for a few days, but I could not go. I had already planned to meet Tim, my old boyfriend, for coffee that week.

By then, too, I had begun taking French lessons with Mademoiselle Millet on Tuesday afternoons. We sat in the dining room and for the first half hour we did grammar. Mademoiselle Millet was adamant about grammar, pronouns, verbs and their conjugation, and feminine and masculine nouns:

La table, le lit . . .

(A table, wooden and solid, should be masculine, a bed, soft and embracing, feminine . . .)

She was also adamant about pronunciation.

"*U*," she said, "*u, u, u.*"

"*Ou, ou,*" I repeated.

If I had gone to Montreal with my husband, I would have had the opportunity to practice my French and see the Rodin exhibit at the Musée des Beaux Arts. According to the museum's website, there were 300 works on loan from the Musée Rodin in Paris, which included the monumental plaster of *The Walking Man*—I watched an online video showing how the museum staff carefully uncrated and assembled the statue. In addition to *The Walking Man*, there were 171 sculptures, sketches, and watercolors, as well as seventy photographs by Eugène Druet in the show. I am especially interested in photography and consider myself a fairly good amateur photographer—before I got married, I saved my money to buy photographs and camera equipment. I would love to have seen those Druet photographs.

Rodin's sculptures reminded me again of poor Camille Claudel.

His daughter often spoke of her. She spoke of her mother in an ordinary way and not in a way to offend or annoy me.

For instance, at dinner one night, his daughter said, "Mom and I went to a movie the other day. We loved it. You should see it," she said turning to me. "The movie or I should say 'film' is Russian. I think it was made years ago—we saw it at Film Forum, where they show old movies. It takes place during World War II and it is incredibly sad. Also, there is this beautiful scene where Boris, the soldier, is shot and as he falls dying, he sees the birch trees turning and spinning above him and—"

"*The Cranes Are Flying*," I said.

"You've seen it then."

"It's one of my favorite films," I told his daughter.

I suggested the park to his son. I suggested
he take his bicycle and told him to ride around on
it while I photographed him with my Rolleiflex 3.5
F. He was very coordinated and he liked to clown.
One of the best photographs I took was of him
standing with one foot on the seat and the other
on the crossbar of his bicycle, his arms spread out,
and laughing.

"I saw this film by Bertolucci," he told me afterward. "It's one of his earliest films, it's called *Before
the Revolution*. Have you seen it?"

I shook my head.

"Anyway, it starts out with this blond guy standing on the seat of his bicycle looking very happy
only he runs into the protagonist of the film and
he falls off his bike. Angry, he gets up and yells at
him: 'And you! What do you think you are doing?
Do you think you are starting a revolution?'"

I like photographing with natural light. I
think it is more flattering and I took photos of his

daughter standing by a window. Mostly head shots. They came out well. It was easy, she was so pretty.

My husband liked the photographs as well. Especially one of his daughter. He asked me to enlarge it and frame it for him, which I did.

"The photograph is on my desk in the office," he told me. "And I tell everyone who comes in and admires it that you took it."

"Shall I make copies of these photographs for your mother?" I asked his daughter.

She hesitated. "Sure," she said. "I think Mom would like to have them."

I put a whole bunch of five-by-eight photos of him riding the bicycle and of her standing by the window in a manila envelope and gave them to his daughter. I wrote her name on the envelope, but I never heard back from her.

The time I dropped off his son's book at her apartment and *she* answered the door in her tai chi outfit, *she* was not looking her best. Her hair was caught up in a messy ponytail and I could see the lines on her face. In a way, I was glad to see her looking older and in slight disarray.

At his daughter's wedding, *she* was wearing a beautiful shiny gray—more like silver—silk suit. It was beautifully cut and it looked expensive. When *she* got up to dance with my husband, *she* took off the jacket and, underneath it, *she* was wearing a cream-colored tank top and her arms were bare.

> *You're just too good to be true*
> *Can't take my eyes off of you*

At the dinner party where we first met, my husband had complimented me on my outfit—the black tuxedo trousers with the satin stripe down the side and the white silk blouse. He was friendly and, unlike most men I know, he asked me about myself and what I did. I told him I worked in marketing but had just been laid off—I did not tell him why—and that I was looking for another job.

"Oh," he said. "Maybe I can help."

In the *New York Times*, I read that Seymour Lipkin, the pianist and conductor—her teacher at the Curtis Institute of Music—died on November 16 in Blue Hill, Maine, at the age of eighty-eight. In the obituary, Margalit Fox wrote: "Underpinning Mr. Lipkin's music-making was his intense sense of communion with the works he performed. That communion was often rooted in deeply personal dialogues he held with composers—exchanges that required only Mr. Lipkin to be present.

"In an interview with the *Philadelphia Enquirer* in 2012, he recounted one especially productive conversation:

> *Beethoven: Lipkin! Make a sforzando here!*
> *Lipkin: Ludwig, I don't feel like it!*
> *Beethoven: Shut up and do what I tell you!*

To his credit, and to the plaudits of critics, Mr. Lipkin generally did."

Had *she* heard?
Did *she* read the newspaper? The obituaries?
Should I call and tell her?

There is a video recording on YouTube of Seymour Lipkin playing Chopin's Nocturne in F Sharp Major, Op. 15, No. 2.

Eighty-six years old at the time, Seymour Lipkin played with great tranquility and nobility. His head slightly bent, his body quite still, he performed without ostentation or flamboyance. Once or twice, he put his left hand on his lap while he played with only his right. He made playing the piano look both natural and impossibly difficult.

I watched the video three times and, despite my tin ear, each time I felt transported.

And did *she*, I had to wonder, play the Chopin nocturne?

On a few Saturday afternoons during the fall, while my husband was either out of town or too busy, I used to drive his son to soccer practice. The soccer field was a few miles outside the city and, depending on traffic, it usually took us about forty-five minutes to get there. At first, we did not say much to each other except for my asking the usual questions in an attempt to make friendly conversation:

"What position do you play?"

"Defense."

"Is soccer your favorite sport?"

"No, not really."

"What is your favorite sport?"

"I don't know. I like skiing."

"And what else?" I asked

"I like tennis."

"So do I," I told him.

"Did you watch the U.S. Open?" I also asked.

"Yeah—it was great."

"Who did you want to win? Nadal or Federer?"

"Rafa."

"Oh, I was hoping Federer would win," I said.

"Yeah, I like Roger, too."

"He's so elegant," I said. "But Nadal is so handsome. Handsome like you," I added.

Also an avid tennis player, my husband had a foursome once a week on Thursday mornings early. The foursome never varied and, according to my husband, they had been playing together for nearly fifteen years. The men played at a club located in midtown—the same club where my husband's daughter's wedding reception took place—and since my husband left his racket, sneakers, and tennis whites in a locker there, he went directly from the club to his office after the game, and after, I presume, a shower.

The men my husband played tennis with were named Stan, David, and Herbie. I met Stan and David and they were both nice enough, but I never got to meet Herbie. Herbie was my husband's doubles partner. One time, when Herbie left a message on our answering message saying that something had come up and he could not play tennis on Thursday, I got to hear his voice.

"Where is he from?" I asked my husband.

"He's from Virginia," my husband answered. "Why do you ask?"

"No reason. Just curious," I said.

"I liked his accent," I also said.

"Now we'll have to get the pro to fill in for him on Thursday," my husband said.

Herbie was the name of my landlord before I got married, when I lived in what was called a "railroad flat" in a town house in the East Village. I had moved there before the area became trendy and my rent was relatively cheap and, more important, stabilized. A ground-floor apartment—nothing fancy, but comfortable—that had a bedroom, a good-sized living room, a dining area, and a small serviceable kitchen. But the best thing about it was that it had access to the garden in the back. In the fall, I planted dozens of tulips that bloomed miraculously every spring and I even bought a rickety old secondhand table and a set of plastic chairs to put out there. In the summer, after work, I often invited friends and colleagues to come over—Herbie, too, and his wife, Miranda, came over a couple of times. We had drinks sitting outside and, often too, we ordered Chinese or Thai food and stayed out late. The garden was quiet and peaceful and it did not feel like the city but like country.

Tim looked the same—maybe he had gained a bit of weight—and he still had all his hair. We talked about old times—our misspent youth in New Orleans—and then we caught up.

"I have three kids," Tim told me. "Two are twins. And you?"

I shook my head. "I have two stepkids. And your wife?"

"Amy. She's a nurse practitioner."

"And what brings you to the city?"

"The boat show." Tim laughed. "Didn't I ever tell you that my dream is to sail around the world?"

I shook my head. "Solo?"

"Yes, unless you come with me."

For old times' sake, I told myself.
No regrets.
Sleeping with Tim was familiar.

I tried asking my husband about his old girlfriends—girlfriends before he got married to her. Usually, I would ask after dinner and after we both had had a few glasses of wine and were mellow.

"So who was your first girlfriend?"

"Who did you lose your virginity to?"

My husband laughed, pleased at the attention, pleased to be able to remember.

"The babysitter" he answered. "When I was twelve."

"Twelve? You must be kidding," I said.

"Maybe I was a bit older—thirteen, fourteen."

"What was her name? The babysitter?"

"Rosemary. Rosemary Fitzpatrick. She was Irish."

"A Catholic?"

My husband shrugged.

"And who was next?" I asked.

And during those same evenings after dinner when we both had drunk too many glasses of wine, I also wanted to ask him:

And who do you love best? Me or her? And who fucks best, me or her?

"My beauty" was what my husband sometimes called me—*ma belle!*

In the photo of her pushing the baby carriage down Avenue Foch in Paris, it was hard to tell—even with a magnifying glass—whether *she* looked happy. But my guess was that *she* was not happy. A new baby, a stubborn little dog, a foreign country, a preoccupied husband . . .

The first time I called her—I called her from a phone booth so *she* could not trace the call—*she* picked up right away and I hung up. The second time, the phone rang several times until her voice mail picked up: *Leave a message and I will call you back as soon as I can,* I heard her say.

His son had her nose, the Grecian nose, like Michelangelo's *David*. But aside from that he did not look like her. He was dark and *she* was blond. A good-looking boy and it was probably a mistake to have told him he was handsome. Instead of complimenting him, I had embarrassed him.

"Self-confidence is important," I told my husband in order to justify myself.

And David put his hand in his bag, and took thence a stone, and slang it, and smote the Philistine in his forehead, that the stone sunk into his forehead; and he fell upon his face to the earth.

Happy birthday, stepmother!
I haven't any money to buy you a present, but I'll
study hard and be first in my class, and that will be
my present. You're the best and the fairest one of all,
and I dream of you every night.
Happy birthday again!

Alfonso

On the first page of his novel, *In Praise of the Stepmother*, Mario Vargas Llosa has the devious little stepson write a letter to his stepmother, Lucrecia, on her fortieth birthday.

According to the *Daily Mail*, five years after he won the Nobel Prize in 2010, Mario Vargas Llosa, aged seventy-nine, left Patricia, his wife of fifty years, for former Filipino beauty queen and socialite Isabel Preysler, saying: "I'm done. Now I feel what happiness is. I don't have much time left."

Marina and I worked in the same office and we often shared properties and clients. Instead of getting a job in marketing, I had gotten my real estate license. It was not a job I felt passionate about, but it was a job that gave me some income and some freedom, and where I could meet people. Marina had grown up in the Czech Republic; there she had met, married, and later divorced an American who had brought her to the States. She was young and lively and we became friends. She told stories about how, in Prague as a child, she joined her parents in the demonstrations that led to the Velvet Revolution. She told how her mother was a good friend of Václav Havel's wife, Olga Splichalova, a charismatic and dashing actress, whom Václav Havel married in 1964.

"Olga was the heroine of the Czech Republic. She was an activist and she was tireless. She also founded a charity to help disabled people, especially the elderly and children. It still exists today," Marina said proudly.

"Have you ever read Václav's *Letters to Olga*—the essays he wrote to her from prison?"

I shook my head.

"She was the most wonderful person I have ever met and I will never forget her," Marina continued.

"Was she beautiful?" I asked.

"She was striking looking but I would not say beautiful. Also, she had lost four fingers in her left hand in an accident—the reason perhaps she was so intent on helping the handicapped."

"What kind of accident?" I asked Marina.

"As a young girl she worked in a factory and she lost her fingers operating a machine."

"Awful," I said, shaking my head again.

"Yes, but that never stopped her. I remember that you hardly noticed her missing fingers. And she never mentioned it. She was a brave woman. Also an understanding one." Marina gave a laugh.

"How do you mean?"

"Václav was a famous womanizer. Olga accepted that. Apparently, when Václav was in prison, she used to joke that at least she knew where he was."

I closed the four fingers of my left hand, leaving out my thumb.

Difficult to imagine.

After Olga Splichalova died in 1996, Václav Havel married Dagmar Veškrnová, an actress, in 1997.

When Marina and I were together, I noticed that I thought about her less often. *She* was not part of our conversation.

All of a sudden, for no apparent reason, I remembered his daughter's husband's uncle's name—Jarvis. An odd name which had reminded me of how, in the movie version of Carson McCullers's *The Member of the Wedding*, Julie Harris, who plays Frankie, the awkward, self-deluded twelve-year-old who plans on joining her older sister and the sister's new husband on their honeymoon, says in that peculiar and distinctive way of hers: "'til this afternoon I didn't have a we, but now after seeing Janice and Jarvis, I suddenly realize that the bride and my brother are the we of me." At the wedding reception, I had mentioned this about the name to his daughter's husband's uncle, but he said he had never seen the movie nor read the book.

My sister Eloise called to tell me that her overweight son got into Yale. Early acceptance, she
added.

"Hal Junior wants to study architecture. Lots of
famous architects went to Yale," she said, starting to
list them, "Eero Saarinen, Norman Foster, Richard
Rogers, Charles Gwathmey, Maya Lin, Robert Stern,
he's the dean of the school—"

"I know," I interrupted her.

"We'll be coming East in September," she then
said.

"Let's make a date for dinner," she continued.
"I so enjoyed meeting your husband. Harold, too,
sends him his regards."

His daughter went to Harvard and graduated
magna cum laude; she also got her MBA there as
did her husband, but I did not tell Eloise this.

Ned Rorem, Marion Zarsecsna, Samuel Barber, Lukas Foss, Leonard Bernstein, Peter Serkin, Lang Lang, and Yefim Bronfman were some of the famous alumni of the Curtis Institute of Music in Philadelphia.

(In Philip Roth's novel *The Human Stain,* the narrator describes attending a rehearsal of a Yefim Bronfman concert at Tanglewood:

Then Bronfman appears. Bronfman the brontosaur! Mr. Fortissimo. Enter Bronfman to play Prokofiev at such a pace and with such bravado as to knock my morbidity clear out of the ring. He is conspicuously massive through the upper torso, a force of nature camouflaged in a sweatshirt, somebody who has strolled into the Music Shed out of a circus where he is the strongman and who takes on the piano as a ridiculous challenge to the gargantuan strength he revels in. Yefim Bronfman looks less like the person who is going to play the piano than like the guy who should be moving it. I had never before seen anybody go at a piano like this sturdy little barrel of an unshaven Russian Jew. When he's finished, I thought, they'll have to throw the thing out. He crushes it. He doesn't let that piano conceal a thing. Whatever's in there is going to come out, and come out with its hands in the air. And when it does, everything there out in the open, the last of the last pulsation, he himself gets up and goes, leaving behind him our redemption. With a jaunty wave, he is suddenly gone, and though he takes all his fire off with him like no less a force than Prometheus, our own lives now seem inextinguishable. Nobody is dying, nobody—not if Bronfman has anything to say about it!)

Marina and I rode down in the elevator with Philip Roth. We had just shown an apartment that was for sale in the building—apparently Philip Roth owned one in the building as well. He gave Marina and me a brief look of appraisal and Marina smiled at him. For a moment Philip Roth hesitated—Marina was good looking.

"What perfume are you wearing?" Philip Roth asked her.

"Shalimar," Marina answered.

Then, turning away, he ignored us both completely. When the elevator reached the ground floor and the doors opened, he got out first.

"Rude," Marina said.

"Misogynist," I said.

Although I caught only a glimpse of her apartment through the open front door when I delivered her son's book, I remembered it distinctly. It was airy and uncluttered and all white. In fact, it was exactly the kind of apartment I would like to have had instead of one filled with old-fashioned antique dark furniture that belonged to my husband's family. In retrospect, I wished I had accepted her invitation and had gone in for a minute. We might have sat down next to each other on the sofa and chatted about ordinary things—the love affair between Nelson Algren and Simone de Beauvoir.

I'm so pleased your daughter is doing so well at Harvard.

Yes, she seems to like her courses a lot.

Once a month, my husband sent her a check for alimony. I never knew for how much. (I tried looking through his checkbook but the check was sent from his office and from a separate bank account.) I did not ask. After all, it was none of my business. And anyway, where money was concerned, my husband was always generous. Among the many presents he gave me, my favorite was a Burmese sapphire from Tiffany.

"For *ma belle!*"

She, I noticed right away, did not wear rings.

Pianists, I have been told—except perhaps
Liberace—rarely wear jewelry when they play.

"Will your mother get married again?" I had asked his daughter.

"No," his daughter answered right away, shaking her head. "I don't think so."

"Does she go out—out with men, I mean?" I persisted.

"She has this one guy, she sees."

"Oh," I said.

"She's known him for a long time. They go on vacations together."

"Where do they go?"

"To the Caribbean mostly, and last year they went to France. To the Dordogne. He rented a castle."

"He must be rich," I said.

His daughter shrugged. "He's nice."

"Is he a musician?"

"No. He's a lawyer. He's older."

*Set in the heart of the beautiful Dordogne coun-
tryside, the château dates back to the fourteenth century
and has remained in the same family all those years.
The château sits on a private estate of 200 hectares of
lawns, meadows, and woodlands, and is located twenty-
five minutes from the market town and capital of the
Dordogne, Périgueux.*

*Périgueux is a particularly charming market town
full of amenities that include supermarkets, cafés, bars,
and a host of excellent restaurants.*

*Nearby the town of Les Eyzies-de-Tayac-Sireuil is
an archaeologist's paradise with many caves containing
prehistoric paintings and deposits.*

Surely *she* must have gone to Les Eyzies-de-Tayac-Sireuil, where, in 1868, Louis Lartet, a geologist, discovered five Cro-Magnon skeletons, one of the earliest examples of *Homo sapiens*; and surely, too, *she* must have visited the Musée nationale de Préhistoire dedicated to the history of the Neanderthals.

And, on the way back to the fourteenth-century château, did *she* and the rich lawyer stop off and dine at a Michelin-starred restaurant in Périgueux?

Deux personnes pour dîner à huit heures.

"Do you like foie gras?" I asked his son, as I put some slices I had bought into the refrigerator.

He made a face. "They force-feed the geese, don't they?"

"It's called *gavage*," I said. "We once ran an ad for a poultry farm in upstate New York that made pâtés and first I had to look up all that stuff to make sure they did not force-feed their ducks."

"And did they?"

"Apparently they did. Someone from an animal anticruelty society took an undercover video that showed the workers shoving tubes down the ducks' throats and one of the workers was quoted as saying: 'Sometimes the duck doesn't get up and dies.' We had to remove our ad."

His son laughed, then he said, "I'm seriously considering becoming a vegetarian."

"I hope you are not a vegetarian," I said to Marina, who was having dinner with us, as I handed her a plate of foie gras and toast.

"I've never been to the Czech Republic," my husband was saying to her, "and Prague sounds like a city full of history."

At first, I understood my husband to say to Marina, "Prague is a city full of *mystery*," not "full of history."

In an interview Václav Havel described the censorship imposed on his letters during the three and half years he spent in prison:

"We were allowed to write one four-page letter home a week. It had to be legible, with nothing corrected or crossed out, and there were strict rules about margins and graphic and stylistic devices (we were forbidden, for example, to use quotation marks, to underline words, use foreign expressions, etc.) . . . We could write only about 'family matters.' Humor was banned as well . . . the reason my letters are so deadly serious."

Despite the differences in their backgrounds, Havel was totally dependent on his wife, Olga: *"In Olga, I found exactly what I needed: someone who could respond to my own mental instability, to offer sober criticism of my wilder ideas, provide private support for my public adventures. All my life, I've consulted with her in everything I do. She's usually the first to read whatever I write, and if not, then she's certainly my main authority when it comes to judging it."*[1]

Havel's letter to her from prison dated August 11, 1979:

Dear Olga,

It's Saturday at five o'clock. I've already had supper and I'm drinking juice and wondering what you're doing. Most likely you're sitting in the yard (Václav and Olga owned a farmhouse in Hrádeček)—*with some friends, I hope—drinking coffee and thinking about moving into the kitchen to light the stove and make supper. I have to fill in the details of your life like this because I have no authentic news at all.*

And again from a letter dated November 3, 1979:

We've survived a lot already and we'll survive this too. We each have our own basket of worries and we'll each have to work through it in our own way. Above all, we must support, not depress, each other. I don't underestimate your worries in the least, and in some regards it will be harder for you than for me.

1. From an interview with Karel Hvížďála, published in Czech in *Dálkovy vyslech* (Purely, Surrey, England: Rozmluvy, 1986).

And from still another letter dated New Year's Eve, 1979:

Dear Olga,

Your visit left me feeling wonderful and I think it was very successful. You looked pretty (!) and it suited you, you radiated serenity, poise and purposeful energy, told me many important things—in short I was exceptionally pleased with you. It seems that this time being a grass widow has been good for you; this temporary emancipation from my domination is allowing you to develop your own identity.

I began a letter to her:

I want to explain what happened. Two weeks after we met at that dinner party you did not go to, your husband came over to my apartment—a railroad apartment I rented in the East Village. He had offered to help me look for another job in marketing and I was grateful. We sat in the garden and he admired the tulips. He said something about how the tulips were amazing and how he felt he was in Holland or someplace, which made me laugh. I also told him how I had planted them all myself. We drank a glass or two of wine, an expensive French Pouilly-Fuissé I had bought especially for the occasion because I assumed—rightly! —he was a wine connoisseur . . . I broke off writing the letter.

On a different subject, I began another letter
to her:

*I want to explain how on my birthday your son
and I drank a bit too much champagne and smoked a
little* . . . Again, I broke off.

I was fairly certain nothing, or nothing damaging, occurred between his son and me. In any case neither one of us was at fault. Yet I could not help being reminded of Mario Vargas Llosa's novel *In Praise of the Stepmother*. Only, in the novel, things get turned around and the stepson sleeps with his stepmother in order to get rid of her.

I cannot forget how at his son's school graduation, one of his teachers, who must have mistaken
me for her on account of our last names, came up
to me and said:

"Your son is gifted. I don't say that about many
of my students, but your son is truly exceptional.
Oh, by the way, my name is Miss Lafferty. I'm the
mathematics teacher here."

We shook hands and I started to explain that I
was only his stepmother, but she continued and said:

"I've taught at this school for twelve years and
I have rarely had a student as intelligent and as
intuitive as your son. His comprehension of difficult
concepts and theories is quite remarkable. I hope
he continues with his studies. It would be a great
pity if he didn't."

Fortunately, just then, my husband had waved
for me to come over and I said good-bye to Miss
Lafferty.

In 1844, Hermann Günther Grassmann published his masterpiece, *Die lineale Ausdehnungslehre, ein neuer Zweig der Mathematik* (*The Theory of Linear Extension, a New Branch of Mathematics*), creating an entirely new subject, linear algebra:

> *Beginning with a collection of "units" $e_1, e_2, e_3, \ldots$, he effectively defines the free linear space which they generate; that is to say, he considers formal linear combinations $a_1 e_1 + a_2 e_2 + a_3 e_3 + \ldots$ where the a_1 are real numbers, defines addition and multiplication by real numbers (in what is now the usual way) and formally proves the linear space properties for these operations. . . . He then develops the theory of linear independence in a way which is astonishingly similar to the presentation one finds in modern linear algebra texts. He defines the notions of subspace, linear independence, span, dimension, join and meet of subspaces, and projections of elements onto subspaces.*[2]

2. Desmond, Fearnley-Sander, "Hermann Grassmann and the Creation of Linear Algebra," *American Mathematical Monthly* 86(1979): 809–17.

Since his work was either ignored or dismissed during his lifetime, Grassmann turned to another discipline, linguistics.

At dinner Marina told us that the Czech language was a West Slavic language and most closely resembled Slovak, Polish, and Silesian.

"Czech word order is very flexible," she also said.

"Give us an example. Say something in Czech," my husband said.

"*Chci se s tebou taky spát.* I can also say the same thing like this," Marina said laughing. "*Chci s tebou spát taky.*"

"What did you say?" I asked her.

"I said dinner is delicious."

While his daughter was trying on her wedding dress and I was buttoning up the row of tiny silk buttons on the back of the dress, I told her how I had always wanted to go to France and how I was taking French lessons.

"You were born there—right?" I said.

"Yes, but I don't remember anything. We left when I was one year old."

"I saw a photo of your mother pushing you in the baby carriage," I said. "She had a little dog on a leash."

"That was Hector. A wirehaired terrier. We brought him back to the States with us. The most disobedient and stubborn dog in the world, according to my mother," she said.

"I would love to have a dog," I told his daughter.

A little later while I was unbuttoning the row of tiny silk buttons on the back of her wedding dress, his daughter said, "Say something. Say something in French."

"*Je t'aime bien.*"

Another argument my husband and I have had
was over my collection of photographs. I was proud
of the photos and how I had saved enough money
to buy them: a color photo by Harry Callahan of a
pink house in Morocco, a Henri Cartier-Bresson
of a family on a houseboat on the Seine (the man
has his back to the camera and is looking at what
appears to be his wife, who is holding a child in her
arms), a William Wegman of his dog, Fay, standing
on a wooden sawhorse, a photo by André Kertész
of some metal chairs in the Luxembourg Garden,
and several others—and I wanted to hang them up
somewhere. I suggested the dining room instead
of the dreary family portraits.

"No way," he said. "Those have been there
forever."

"Then how about in the library or in the hall
instead of those copies of Piranesi prints?"

"Those aren't copies. They're original prints."

The time my husband came over to my apartment and we drank the expensive Pouilly-Fuissé in the garden before we ended up making love, he had admired the photographs. Instead of hanging them up, I had the framed photos on the floor propped up against the walls—the way I had seen a famous architect's photos displayed in a fashion magazine article—and he had to bend down to get a good look at them.

He wore an expensive-looking tweed jacket and a blue shirt that was open at the collar——on entering the apartment, he had taken off his tie and stuffed it into his jacket pocket—gray slacks, and brown loafers with a high polish.

"I really like this one," he had said, pointing to the Henri Cartier-Bresson photograph, "and I have always wanted to live on a houseboat."

"Me, too," I lied.

The morning I was supposed to meet Marina for breakfast at the new French bakery around the corner from the office, she never showed up. I waited and waited before I finally ordered myself a café au lait and a croissant. Twice, too, I tried calling her, first at home, then on her cell phone, but each time there was no answer.

I have forgotten how, at dinner, we got onto the subject, but, turning to me, Marina had corrected my pronunciation: "duh-VOR-jacque—" she said.

"Dvořák is my favorite composer," she added. "Of course, because he is Czech and as a child I used to play the violin. Badly," she added, smiling.

"What about you?" she asked my husband. "Are you musical?"

"No, not really. But my wife—" He paused, then, looking over at me, he said, "I mean my ex-wife was musical. She played the piano."

Then to lighten the mood, my husband said, "In fourth grade, I played the recorder."

"And who did you sleep with next, after the Irish babysitter?" I asked him one Sunday morning after we had made love.

"Honestly," he answered, still holding me in his arms, "I don't remember."

Then, closing his eyes, he smiled. "You," he said. "I slept with you next."

I remember every man I have ever slept with—good and bad.

After my husband and I first made love and after he left—although it had begun to rain—I went out into the garden and took several photographs of the tulips.

Because I had never planted anything and because I am cautious, I followed the directions to a T:

Plant tulip bulbs in the fall, 6 to 8 weeks before a hard frost is expected

Tulips prefer a site with full or afternoon sun

All tulips dislike excessive moisture. The soil should be well-drained, neutral to slightly acidic

Space bulbs 4 to 6 inches apart

Plant bulbs deep—at least 8 inches, measuring from the base of the bulb

Set the bulb in the hole with the pointy end up

Water bulbs right after planting to trigger their growth

Detained out of town, my husband sent a beautiful assortment of tulips, lilacs, and peonies for my fortieth birthday.

"I am surprised he remembered," his son, who answered the door and brought in the flowers, said. "Usually he forgets everybody's birthday."

"What about your mother's birthday—when is it?" I asked.

Mario Vargas Llosa's novel also begins on the stepmother's fortieth birthday.

Her birthday is March 5 and *she* is a Pisces. Pisces is a Water sign and the ruling planet is Neptune. Neptune is associated with the arts, in particular with music! People born under the sign of Pisces are friendly, selfless, compassionate, and wise.

As for me I am a Gemini, an Air sign, and my ruling planet is Mercury. Mercury is associated with aspects of the mind such as communication, writing, and teaching. People born under the sign of Gemini are inquisitive, sociable, and versatile— often showing two sides of their personality.

Often, too, people born under the sign of Gemini feel that their other half is missing and they look for new friends and mentors.

"We should celebrate!" his son had said that evening.

He did not look like my husband, nor did he look like her. Instead he looked a lot like Rafael Nadal—his thick dark hair, his sturdy limbs.

Bored pushing the big old-fashioned baby carriage down Avenue Foch, exasperated pulling stubborn Hector on the leash, frustrated waiting for her husband to come home late from INSEAD, did *she* have an affair with an elegant, dark-haired Frenchman with a patrician-sounding double name— *Jean-Pierre, Jean-Marc . . . ?*

His daughter, on the other hand, looked exactly like my husband, only she was lovely.

"Happy birthday!" His daughter telephoned me.

"Is Dad there?" she also had said. "Can I speak to him?"

"Your father's flight from Seattle was canceled on account of bad weather," I told her. "He should be home tomorrow."

I didn't want her to be concerned or to think that I was.

His daughter was very intuitive. Like her mother, she was a Pisces.

The boarding pass stub in my husband's coat pocket indicated that he had come not from Seattle but from Chicago's O'Hare International Airport.

"Sorry I missed your birthday," he had said as he walked into the apartment, "and that you were home alone last night."

"I had a good book," I said, not looking at him.

Fortunately, incurious, my husband did not ask me the title of the book or what the book was about. Instead, he asked after his son.

"Is he here?"

From the laundry basket, I sniffed his shirt for the scent of Shalimar.

Along with the story of Alfonso's betrayal, Mario Vargas Llosa included six color illustrations of paintings in *In Praise of the Stepmother*, so as to provide the husband Don Rigoberto and his wife Lucrecia with fantasies during their lovemaking. One painting, *Candaules, King of Lydia, showing his wife to Prime Minister Gyges* by Jacob Jordaens, shows a steatopygous (fat-assed) nude. This painting allows Don Rigoberto to impersonate Candaules and rhapsodize about his wife's buttocks: *Each hemisphere is a carnal paradise; the two of them, separated by a delicate cleft of nearly imperceptible down that vanishes in the forest of intoxicating whiteness, blackness, and silkiness that crowns the firm columns of her thighs* . . .

To celebrate, we had opened a bottle of champagne—*pop!* A 1990 Moët & Chandon Dom Pérignon that my husband kept in the refrigerator for special occasions. We also smoked some pot (I haven't smoked pot since I lived in the rented railroad apartment in the East Village), and we did a few lines of cocaine (I haven't done cocaine since I was a student at Tulane), and we laughed a lot—I don't remember what about—laughed so hard we cried. Afterward, to come down, we each took a Valium.

When I woke up the next morning, his son was gone.

The liquor store was out of the 1990 Dom Pérignon when I went to try to replace it. And, anyway, Ken, the salesman, told me, the champagne would have cost me a small fortune.

I could have bought a bottle of Moet & Chandon Brut Imperial for $49.95, but I didn't. Instead when my husband opened the refrigerator and noticed the champagne gone, I told him I gave it to Margarita to celebrate getting her green card.

"You did what? You gave the housekeeper a two-hundred-dollar bottle of champagne!"

We both lied. *Kif-kif,* as the French say.

Ken, the liquor store salesman, liked to chat with his customers. He liked telling them little-known facts about the bottles of alcohol they were buying.

"Dom Pérignon champagne is supposed to be named after a Benedictine monk named Pierre Pérignon, but the fact of the matter is that sparkling wine—"

"Sorry, Ken," I interrupted, "I have to run."

Frowning, my husband asked Margarita, "Did you enjoy the champagne?"

Turning off the vacuum cleaner, Margarita stared at him for a moment before she opened her mouth to answer.

"*Sí, señor,*" she said.

Margarita knew enough—even if she did not always understand what was being said to her in English—to know that it was best never to contradict her employer and risk being fired.

Like Mario Vargas Llosa, Margarita was from Peru and, like Vargas Llosa, she was born in Arequipa—the second-largest and southernmost city in Peru—but unlike Vargas Llosa, a descendant of wealthy criollos, Margarita was a descendant of poor mestizos.

"One more thing," my husband continued, holding up his hand to keep Margarita from turning on the vacuum again, "when you went into the bedroom to clean this morning were my wife and my son in the bed together?"

Again Margarita said, "*Sí, señor.*"

I admitted we slept in the same bed (my husband's king-size sleigh bed), but we did not sleep together—we did not fuck.

Filing for a divorce in New York State is a tedious affair despite Governor David Paterson's signing no-fault divorce into law on August 15, 2010. And even if the divorce is uncontested, many court forms must be filled out and filed:

Summons with Notice or Summons and Complaint

Affirmation of Regularity (Form UD-5, which requests that your case be put on the calendar)

Affidavit of Plaintiff (Form UD-6)

Three copies of the Note of Issue (Form UD-9)

Findings of Fact/Conclusions of Law (Form UD-10)

Judgment of Divorce (Form UD-11)

Part 130 Certification (Form UD-12)

Affidavit of Defendant (Form UD-7, if your spouse signed and returned it to you)

Certificate of Dissolution of Marriage

Postcard, and USC 111—Divorce and Child Support Summary Form.

If your spouse did not sign and return the affidavit of defendant, then you must also file:

Affidavit of Service (Form UD-3), and

Sworn Statement of Barriers to Remarriage (Form UD-4).

If you and your spouse have children together, then you also have to file the forms related to child support (Forms UD-8, UD-8a, and UD-8b).

When all the forms are completed and brought to the county clerk's office to file and the filing fees have been paid—unless a waiver has been granted based on income—the clerk will submit the papers to the judge and if the judge approves the paperwork, he or she will issue a judgment of divorce.

The railroad apartment in the East Village is no longer available—and, if it was, the rent, no doubt, would be triple or quadruple . . .

And what about those tulips?

Hello!

This time I won't hang up if *she* picks up the phone.

Or if her voice mail picks up—*Leave a message and I will call you back as soon as I can*—

I will leave a message asking her if *she* will play Chopin's Nocturne in F Sharp Major, Op. 15, No. 2 for me.